MW00906839

SQUIRREL HOTEL

ALSO WRITTEN AND ILLUSTRATED BY

WILLIAM PÈNE DU BOIS

Peter Graves
The Twenty-one Balloons
The Flying Locomotive
The Great Geppy
The Three Policemen

ILLUSTRATED BY

WILLIAM PÈNE DU BOIS

The Witch of Scrapfaggot Green
Harriett

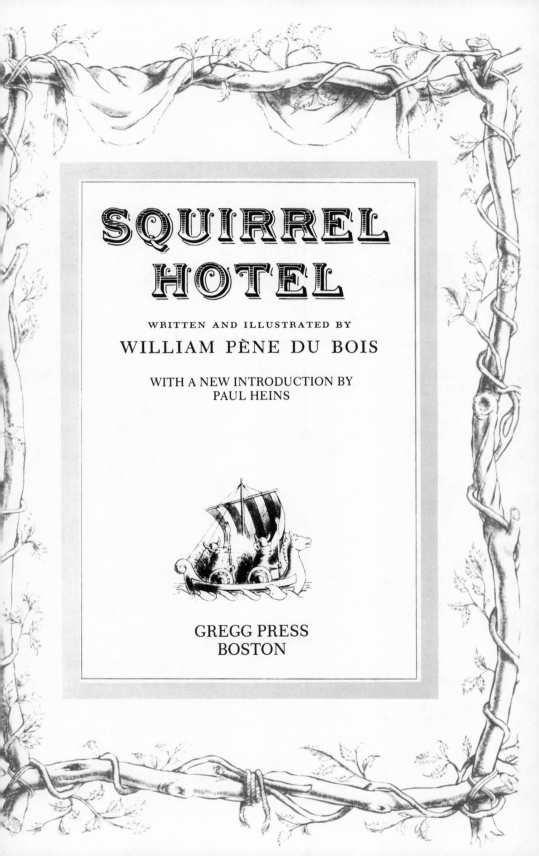

SQUIRREL HOTEL

WRITTEN AND ILLUSTRATED BY

WILLIAM PÈNE DU BOIS

WITH A NEW INTRODUCTION BY
PAUL HEINS

GREGG PRESS
BOSTON

With the exception of the Introduction, this is a complete photographic reprint of a work first published in New York by The Viking Press in 1952.

The trim size of the original hardcover edition was 6¼ by 9⅞ inches.

Gregg Press Children's Literature Series logo by Trina Schart Hyman

Text copyright 1951 William Pène du Bois, renewed 1979

This story originally appeared in *Mademoiselle*

Reprinted by arrangement with the author's agent

Introduction copyright © 1980 by Paul Heins

New material designed by Barbara Anderson

Printed on permanent/durable acid-free paper and bound in the United States of America

Republished in 1979 by Gregg Press, A Division of G.K. Hall & Co., 70 Lincoln St., Boston, Massachusetts 02111

First Printing, January 1980

Library of Congress Cataloging in Publication Data

Du Bois, William Pène, 1916-
    Squirrel Hotel.

    (Gregg Press children's literature series)
    Reprint of the ed. published by Viking Press, New York.
    SUMMARY: A young reporter recounts his brief friendship with an extraordinary man who built the Squirrel Hotel and conducted the Bee Orchestra.
    I. Title. II. Series.
[PZ7.D8527Sq 1979]   [Fic]   79-17958
ISBN 0-8398-2606-0

Introduction

ON THE dust jacket of the original 1938 edition of *The Three Policemen,* there is a photograph with the following legend: "This is William Pène du Bois, the author. . . . He's also the artist who painted and drew all the pictures. He is twenty years old and he likes to write stories almost as well as he likes to draw pictures for them." Actually, he was born in 1916, and it was the original version of *Elizabeth the Cow Ghost* (1936) that was published when he was 20. The photograph, however, belied his age. Extremely youthful in appearance, he appeared boyish — smiling and good-natured, but obviously full of a quiet kind of exuberance. And the books he wrote and illustrated in the years before he spent a term in the United States Army were to reflect his spontaneous ingenuity and power of invention. He knew how to begin a story, and his opening sentences were happy combinations of precision and fantasy. *The Three Policemen* begins, "In the Atlantic Ocean there is an island known to few people called Farbe Island (n. lat. 58°, w. long. 16°) which is shaped like a fish" (p. 7); and *The Flying Locomotive* (1941) is launched thus: "At exactly 2.24 o'clock, June 3, 1909, two magnificent locomotives were completed at the railway yards of Basel, in Switzerland" (p. 5).

William Pène du Bois, whose ancestors originally came to New Orleans in 1738, was born in New Jersey, the son of a painter and art critic. Educated in France between the ages of eight and fourteen, he became imbued with the Gallic spirit and developed three enthusiasms: the homeland of his ancestors, French circuses, and the works of Jules Verne. His drawing was influenced, he tells us in his Newbery Acceptance speech, by his father and by M. Dirémaire, the arithmetic teacher at the Lycée Hoche, a boarding school in Versailles, where the discipline was "far more frightening and regimented than that of the United States Army." M. Dirémaire was as interested in the appearance of the arithmetic papers as in their contents and frowned on lines drawn freehand.

In 1947, after five years in the army, William Pène du Bois wrote and illustrated a more extended work than he had hitherto attempted: *The Twenty-One Balloons* (1947). This book, which received the Newbery Medal, marked a development in both his writing and his drawing. Or rather a maturing: for — always interested in islands and modes of transportation — he had already written an island story in *The Three Po-*

licemen and had invented and diagrammed a remarkable vehicle in the shape of a sea serpent in the same book. During the next ten years he went on to produce two other works which embodied a disciplined and logical sense of fantasy: *Squirrel Hotel* (1952) and *Lion* (1956). *Lion* may be called a metaphysical fantasy. Set in a heavenly workshop, where angels are busy creating animals, the book dramatizes the genesis of Lion's correct form and voice. Needless to say, the absurd ineptitude of the first unsuccessful attempts of Artist Foreman to match the image and the word is part of the fun — of both the visual and the intellectual fun of the book.

Squirrel Hotel is almost in a class by itself, but it does have strong ties with *Lion* and with *The Twenty-One Balloons*. Unlike them, it is told completely as a first-person story. Extremely orderly on the surface, it is divided into a four-part narrative, reminding one of du Bois's use of precise alphabetical arrangements in both *Lion* and *The Twenty-One Balloons*. The rationale of how the old man taught bees to produce music and the description of the construction and of the elaboration of Squirrel Hotel suggest the scientific pragmatism of Jules Verne. But the story ends with a teasing incompleteness; and unlike *Lion* and *The Twenty-One Balloons*, which are ebullient and joyous, *Squirrel Hotel* is slightly tinged with melancholy and redolent of mystery.

What is most remarkable about *Squirrel Hotel*, however, is the form of the plot. The events are carefully generated. The first-person narrator opens by saying, "I once met an old man, a terribly old man, who told me a secret which I promised not to tell anyone" (p. 7), and immediately — in the opening paragraph — lets the reader know about the existence of Squirrel Hotel. He tells how he met the old man — accidentally, as it were — when he went to the park to watch children sailing toy boats and "strange old mechanics" with "remarkable homemade steam or gasoline motorboats" (p. 8). By chance, he finds a crowd around the old man and his Bee Orchestra, becomes acquainted with him, wins his confidence, and is finally accosted with the question "Do you like squirrels?" (p. 17). In the course of the next few days, the 80-year-old man tells of his retirement from the toy business, of his building a magnificent structure for squirrels to live in, and promises the narrator, "Young man, come and see me again tomorrow. I shall take you to Squirrel Hotel and turn the place over to you" (p. 40).

But on the next day the old man doesn't turn up; he never appears again, and the narrator as well as the reader has reasons to doubt the veracity of the octogenarian. The young man does some detective work; he visits the toy shop and finds that Mr. Leonard Schurman, the former proprietor, had purchased many miniature items that could have been used to furnish a miniature hotel.

The narrator's final statements are poignantly logical.

> If someone had told me of the Bee's Orchestra and of Squirrel Hotel I would have found it far easier to believe in the existence of Squirrel Hotel.
> But *I have seen* the Bee's Orchestra.

> Please help me find Squirrel Hotel, or if you have seen it, please tell me where it is. It most probably needs a good deal of attention and care, and I *am* supposed to be the person left in charge. (p. 48)

The strangest thing of all is that we have seen Squirrel Hotel on the pages of the book. All the illustrations, except for the drawing of Grock, the Swiss clown, are of animals and objects rather than of people. The characters — and the old man is a tantalizing creation — appear only in the words of the story in which the carefully described mechanical details and pictures give verisimilitude to a fantasy that is so realistic and logical that one feels it to be a presentation of actuality. Thus the author-illustrator balances possibility and improbability, creating not only amazement but pathos — the pathos of unattainability.

Paul Heins
Auburndale, Massachusetts

TO MY GOOD FRIENDS
BARBARA AND LEONARD

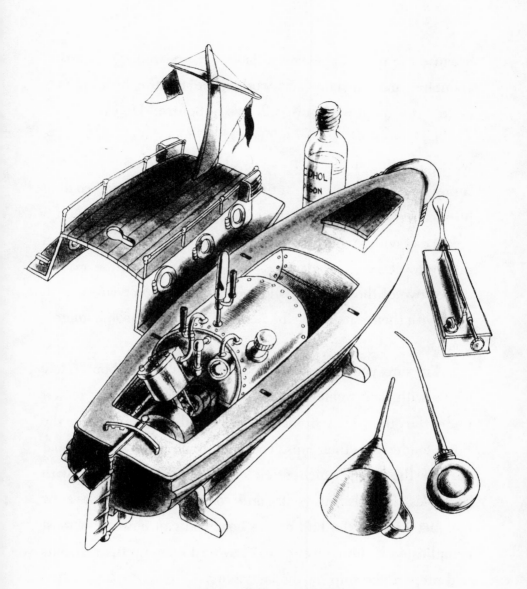

THE FIRST DAY

I once met an old man, a terribly old man, who told me a secret
which I promised not to tell anyone. This was over three years
ago. I haven't told his secret until now. I'm going to tell it now

because the old man seems to have disappeared. I'm worried about him and the many hard-working and trusting little animals he told me about who must still live in Squirrel Hotel.

To begin with, I must tell you how I met the old man. This was interesting in itself. I was walking through the park one sunny day in August, a beautiful clear day with a nice cooling breeze. I was heading for the lake, for I knew that on such a lovely day with such a nice wind there would be a lot of children sailing toy boats, and perhaps—and this interested me more— one or two of those strange old mechanics who appear on such days with their remarkable homemade steam or gasoline motor-boats.

I'm sure you've seen the fellows I'm writing about. They arrive with their model boats under one arm and a big toolkit under the other. They sit on a bench near the lake and place the boats tenderly on their laps. They first remove the whole upper part of the boat, which often consists of little cabins with portholes, funnels, air vents, and sometimes even little crew members. Inside the hull of the boat you can now see a most complicated handmade engine. They next open up their toolkits and prepare the ship for the launching.

Their toolkits are always the same. They are the type with three trays which spread out like magic when the lid is lifted. The trays contain old and worn tin boxes full of collections of odd nuts and bolts and small metalware. There are rags in them too, and little bottles of wood alcohol or gasoline, little

funnels, and long pointed pincers, tiny screwdrivers, and grace-
ful tack hammers. I won't waste more time on these fellows, for
if you live in the city I'm certain you've seen them.

They spend about two hours and three-quarters getting
the boat ready. Next, fifteen minutes or so in a tremendous effort
to get the boat, which is now spitting steam or tiny gas explo-
sions, to move when dunked in the water. Then, before going
home, they spend another two hours and three-quarters drying
and cleaning the boat off with the old rags.

In spite of this slow procedure, these fellows manage to
gather a quiet little crowd of people who follow with extraordinary interest every move they make. The people who spend so
much time watching them must all be lazy fools with nothing
better to do. I am one of these; so I headed for the lake on this
warm and breezy day.

You can easily spot homemade motorboaters by the little
crowds they gather. You can imagine how excited I was when,
on reaching the top of the hill overlooking the lake, I saw about
fifty people surrounding someone seated on a bench. I also saw
a familiar steamboater seated all alone and unwatched on
another bench nearby. This fellow usually had an audience of
between fourteen and eighteen people. I was sure that the man
with the crowd had something fabulous to display, perhaps a
model of the *Queen Mary* with four complicated engines to
operate each of the four propellers, and a toolkit with six pop-up
trays. I hurried down the hill to the bench.

9

As I approached it, a peculiar buzzing sound came to my ears. I rubbed them briskly, trying to clear away this sound, but as I neared the crowd the sound seemed to get just a tiny bit louder. I suddenly recognized the melody of the "Skater's Waltz" played ever so softly with a delicate mixing of this buzzing sound and the tinkle of tiny bells. I thought at first that this must be music from the world's smallest violin. I've heard the world's smallest violin played by Grock, the famous Swiss clown, in Paris. I interviewed Grock after the performance for a newspaper article. He told me that he bought it from a famous violin maker on Bond Street in London. He said he had paid seven dollars and fifty cents for it and had since played it in every country in the world. Because he had made it so famous, the same violin maker who sold it to him offered to buy it back for one thousand dollars. He wanted to put it, with its tiny old plush and leather case, in the middle of his store window. Grock told me he wouldn't sell it for three times that amount. I know Grock doesn't play it on park benches, so this couldn't have been music from the world's smallest violin.

The crowd was so thick around the bench that I couldn't see how the music was made. The "Skater's Waltz" ended gracefully and received a loud burst of applause. It was then that I first saw the old man. It was apparently he who had been making the music. He was passing a hat amongst his admirers to collect money for his performance. It was while he was doing this that I managed, rather rudely, to push my way through

Grock

William Pène du Bois , Paris

the crowd closer to the bench. I did this by fumbling clumsily in my pockets for money when he stood before me with his hat, not finding any, then finding some, and following him through the crowd back to the bench to give it to him. Nobody complained at seeing me do this, and I felt rather pleased with the trick. As an encore, the old man played the famous Spanish melody "Marquita."

The instrument the man made the music with was extraordinary. Actually, you couldn't really call it an instrument, for the music was made by sixteen musicians. Instead of coming from the world's smallest violin, this music was made by the world's tiniest orchestra.

This is what it looked like. There was a little long stage, elegantly designed; I should say that it was about four feet long and one foot high. There was a little easel to one side of the stage with the names of the selections printed on little cards. When the curtain parted I saw sixteen tiny wires sticking up from the stage in a straight row and on top of each wire there was a little bell. The bells were different in size. The one on the

left was biggest, and they got smaller and smaller down to the one on the far right, which was indeed tiny. These bells accounted for the tinkling sound—but what made the buzzing sound? What *does* make a buzzing sound? *Bees,* of course! There was a bee attached to each wire by a small thread. There was a huge bumblebee tied to the biggest bell, on the left, and the bees got smaller and smaller down to a flea-sized bee on the right. How was the orchestra directed and the music made? In a most clever way. The old man had in one hand a small and beautiful rose, the smell of which no bee could resist. On his other hand he wore a white cotton glove, delicately perfumed with kerosene, the smell of which no bee could possibly stand. He would move the rose close to the nose of the bee who

13

made the proper buzz sound, and the bee would fly furiously toward it, ringing his little bell and buzzing clearly. While this bee was performing, playing his one particular note, the old man kept a sharp eye on the other bees, gently waving the kerosened glove in front of them to keep them quiet. He passed his rosè and glove from bee to bee, and thus the charming music was made.

There was a foot pedal beneath the stage, and when he pushed this down a partition covered with felt would rise the length of the stage, behind the wires, holding the bells still so that only the delicate sound of the bees could be heard. I can't ever remember before having come across such a delightful and enchanting orchestra.

You may have gathered that I occasionally write articles for newspapers. I fairly shook with excitement at the prospect of interviewing the old man. It seemed to me that here was a strange story which any newspaper would snatch up quickly, no matter how badly it was told. I was determined to meet the old man and hoped above hope that I might be the first person who thought of writing about him.

"Marquita" was the last selection of the concert. The old

man bowed to the enthusiastic hand he received. He then made the following remarkable little speech:

"Ladies and Gentlemen, we thank you for your generous response. Our little concert is over. I am about to turn the tired musicians loose. Musicians are famous for being nervous and highly strung; my musicians are particularly temperamental. This is in way of a warning. I myself have . . ." But that was as far as he got, for, as he took a pair of scissors out of his pocket, the crowd instantly dispersed in all directions. I ran with the rest and was fifty yards away from the old man in no time; then I stopped short and walked back to his bench. I suddenly thought that his story was surely worth a bee sting.

He had cut his orchestra loose; there wasn't a bee in sight! He unhooked the sides of his little stage, swung them back on hinges, and the whole thing folded flat. He took the cards off the easel and put them in one pocket, folded the easel and put it in another, and started to walk off. I quickly asked him if he would mind sitting down on the bench and talking with me for a while.

"Of course not. Why should I?" he answered.

I thanked him. I then asked him if he had any objections to getting a bit of free publicity.

"What for?" he asked.

"It might increase the size of your audiences and the amount of money your receive."

"The stage is too small," he said. "I can handle only fifty

15

people at the most, and so far I've had no trouble in getting them. As for money"—his face broke out into a broad grin—"listen to this!" He shook his pocket. "Let's count it, shall we?" He pulled out a fistful of coins and a carefully folded dollar or two. He slowly added it up. "Fourteen dollars and thirty-five cents. Not bad, eh? That's about ninety-eight dollars a week if I work every day."

"Do you work every day?"

"I intend to for a while."

"How many concerts have you given so far?"

"This was my first."

"This is amazing," I said. "But you've just cut your orchestra loose. How will you perform tomorrow?"

"I'll get up a new orchestra, of course."

"But why did you get rid of the old one?"

"I had to. The smaller bees are just growing babies; they go out of tune overnight. They're like children whose voices are changing, only their notes change much quicker. Besides, I'm sure the Society for Prevention of Cruelty to Animals would get angry if I didn't set them free after five or six numbers."

"Where do you get the bees?"

"A friend of mine raises them. He sells them to me at cost price, which is quite cheap indeed. It takes me about two hours to set up a new orchestra. I use tuning forks. Two hours to set it up, a half-hour for a full concert, and I'm through for the day. Why should I need publicity?"

"Have you thought of television?"

"Bah!" he said. "Young man, this Bee Orchestra isn't my whole life or my only interest, not by any means."

"What is your main interest?"

"I've never told *that* to anyone." As the old man said this he looked at me in a strange way that suggested that he might possibly tell it to me. "What do *you* do for a living?"

"I'm a writer at times," I answered, "and I sometimes do illustrations, mostly for magazines."

"Have you a good imagination? Or what sort of writing do you do?"

"Unfortunately I'm afraid it's mostly factual, newspaper reporting and such." I suddenly found myself being interviewed.

"Oh," he said. He seemed quite disappointed. "Do you work on a newspaper?"

"No, my time is quite my own."

"*Good!*" he shouted. "I don't like regular working hours, do you?"

I smiled and agreed.

"Do you like squirrels?" he asked.

"Why, yes, I certainly do."

"Do you really like squirrels?"

"Very much," I said earnestly.

"Well, I'm the operator of—that is, I'm the manager of—" He hesitated a long time.

"Go on," I said reassuringly. "We have one definite thing

in common which seems to be important. We *both* like squirrels!"

"I really don't know whether I should tell my secret," he said, "but my friends, what few friends I have, all have dreadful boring jobs with regular working hours. I have a feeling that I haven't much longer to live. I need someone to take over. I would like to show him how now."

"I am very good at keeping secrets," I said.

"Well, I am the manager of a most extraordinary establishment." He looked to each side to make sure we were alone. "I'm the only man who knows about it. It's called Squirrel Hotel." His voice faded off to a whisper. "I must go now," he added. "If you are really interested in knowing about it, if your liking of squirrels is really genuine, come and see me again tomorrow at this time, at this same bench, and I'll tell you a little about it. I'll tell you a little more day by day. I want to make certain that you are really interested."

"I most certainly will be here," I said.

"Good!" he said. "Very good. I have a feeling I can trust you." We shook hands rather hastily. I noticed that his hands were quite bumpy. I wondered as I walked off what those bumps could be, but then, of course, I quickly guessed what they were—they were bee stings.

I scratched my head, pinched myself to make sure I wasn't dreaming, and walked home. Before going to bed, I made a drawing of the Bee Orchestra from memory, and I wrote a few notes about it for a possible article.

18

THE SECOND DAY

Of course I kept my appointment and was happy to see that
the old man had attracted an even bigger audience than the
day before. I recognized a few faces in the group and guessed
that these people were so enchanted by yesterday's concert that
they had returned with friends.

The old man didn't disappoint them one bit. He played an entirely different program and, after passing the hat, topped everything I'd heard him play till then with a most stirring rendition of the Army Air Corps song. This was played with the foot pedal down so that there was no tinkling sound from the bells. He directed the orchestra with several roses, so that the buzzing was more furious than before. After reaching the final martial note, he quickly produced a handful of flowers, which he spread out in front of the bees. This produced a loud buzzing chord like the sound of a tiny air squadron; but this wasn't all. He reached in his pockets for two felt-lined wooden boxes, opened them, and took from them two tiny drums which he placed at each end of the stage. These drums were beating frantically, apparently from the action of some small being inside them. After allowing the sound of the self-beating drums to mingle a few moments with the throbbing chord of the buzzing bees, he waved his kerosened glove for quiet. He silenced the bees and removed the roses. He opened the drums, from which flew forth two handsome dragonflies with tiny silk American flags attached to their tails. The crowd cheered and applauded and followed the dragonflies with their eyes. The insects flew off with such great speed they managed to shake the flags from their tails. These dropped gently into the outstretched fingers of the children in the audience who had scampered off to catch them. With the children out of the way, the old man bowed and, without bothering to repeat his little closing speech of the day before, quickly cut the Bee Orchestra loose. The crowd dispersed, and I approached him as he was folding up the little stage.

"Hello," I said. "As you can see, I've kept my appointment."

"Appointment for what?" he asked.

I gulped slightly at the abruptness of his question, then said, "I saw you yesterday. We had a little talk. You said that if I were really interested to come back today."

"I recognize your face," he said, "but what were we to talk about?" He looked beyond me and to each side of me and behind himself as he asked this.

"Squirrel Hotel," I replied in a low voice.

"Ah, Squirrel Hotel," he whispered, smiling. "Sit down, then. A most remarkable establishment, if I do say so myself. Yes, yes, sit down. I'll tell you a little more about it."

"I beg your pardon, sir," I said, "but so far you have told me nothing about Squirrel Hotel. I say this only because you say that you are going to tell me a little more. I hope you will start from the beginning."

"*Young man!*" he shouted. "I have told you that Squirrel Hotel exists, which is indeed *something*. You and I are the only *two* who know of this!"

"I see," I said. "Excuse me for interrupting you."

"As for how the hotel came to be," he continued, "I will, as I said yesterday, tell you every step in small doses to make certain that your interest is sincere."

"Very good, sir."

"First let's count the money. I can't stand the suspense!" He reached in his pockets and pulled forth fistfuls of coins. I helped him total it up. The amount came to sixteen dollars and twenty-eight cents. "Better than yesterday!" he exclaimed. "Fantastic! A little while ago I didn't know how I was going to keep alive. Now I have a reasonable income—most reasonable!"

"A well-deserved one," I remarked.

"Five years and twenty-one days ago, I retired from business on my seventy-fifth birthday. I sold the store and divided all the money I had into five equal portions. I figured that I was going to live until I was eighty, or perhaps not quite so long, and I wanted to have five rich and comfortable years. I was all alone, with no dependents and no responsibilities. Why, I asked myself, plan on ten lean years when I might die bored and depressed in the second or third with a sockful of money raring to be spent? I had five rich years of travel, pleasure, anything I wanted to do—why, in my second year, I bought a second-hand Rolls Royce and followed the circus all over the country. Everything was planned gloriously to end on my eightieth birthday. The money, the lease on my apartment, my life—all were to run out at midnight twenty-one days ago. You can well imagine my chagrin, my perplexity, when, on the morning of the first day of my eightieth year, the time of my planned departure from the earth, I awoke very much alive and kicking. There was something about the silliness of the situation that made me feel healthier and hungrier than ever. I believe I could have stashed away a dozen eggs that morning, without stopping for breath. My furniture and lovely automobile, which I had previously sold, were called for and driven away. My clothes, except for the suit on my back, had been promised to a charity organization which did not fail to pick them up promptly. New tenants came to occupy my rooms. I watched all of my worldly possessions disappear one by one, leaving me only with body and soul, wrapped up in a suit, and a depressingly eager will to live. With the help of the squirrels, I was just about able to get along until I got the idea for this Bee Orchestra—but now I'm getting way ahead of my story."

"Amazing!" I said. "But let's go back to your business. What sort of a store did you own?"

"It was a toy store—perhaps you heard of it. It was called Land, Sea & Air, Inc."

"I can't say that I have. It sounds rather interesting."

"It was quite handsome and pleasant," he said. "There were three rooms. The first one, the Land Room, was painted in shades of brown, beige, and tan. In it were displayed only toys connected with land, such as automobiles, trucks, fire engines, tractors, soldiers, cannons, tanks, derricks, bicycles, trains, steam engines, tunnels, animals, graders, bulldozers, and the like. Being an old landlubber, I handled the Land Room myself. The Sea Room was painted Nile and viridian green. On its lower shelves were submarines and deep-sea divers, diving bells, toy

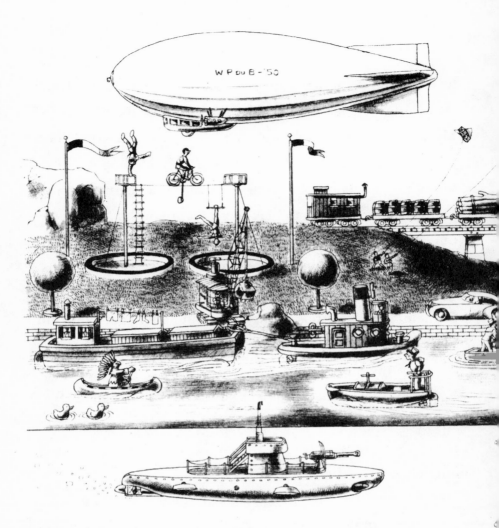

(drawn from the mural in the office of the director of Land, Sea & Air, Inc)

fish, spears, goggles, and fins. The upper shelves were laden with ocean liners, battleships, tugboats, barges, speedboats, sailboats, steamboats, rowboats, rubber horses, alligators, ducks, and so forth; fishing rods, reels, tackle, water bicycles—in short, the sea at its surface. As salesman for the Sea Room I hired the services of a retired sea captain, one Philippe Saalburg, who came complete with peg leg and salty manner. The Air Room

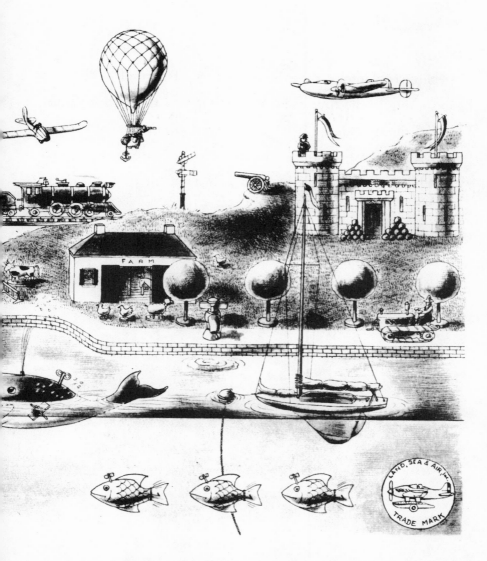

was painted shades of cerulean blue and was filled with model airplanes, balloons and dirigibles, kites and gliders. A Colonel John Philips was in charge, one of the few men in the world who has flown in every form of aircraft. It was quite a fine store, carefully stocked, and I'm most happy to say that I got out of business before the plastic age roared in like a lion."

"I couldn't agree with you more. Now, on to Squirrel Hotel."

"Squirrel Hotel was perhaps a direct offshoot of my having been so long in the toy business. Dealing as I did with models, I always thought that I was going to get around to building a few myself. I never did. This was perhaps because they were so available. Well, one afternoon, an afternoon in the third year after I'd retired from business, I was sitting on a park bench quite like this one, looking up, feeling delighted, and daydreaming about my recent trip following the circus across the country.

I was quite off in a cloud when suddenly I noticed that a small pair of eyes had been looking steadily down at me. There is always a slight feeling of embarrassment when one finds that one isn't quite alone, particularly if one happens to have been grinning broadly, as I was at the time. I self-consciously waved at the pair of eyes, which, by the way, belonged to a young squirrel who had poked his head out of the window of his small tree house. Thinking that I was inviting him down for some kind of a food handout, he ran down the tree and sat on the bench beside me, a pleading look on his small face and his paws across his chest Chinese Mandarin style.

"I didn't have a thing to offer him, and in waving my arms and shrugging my shoulders at him in a pantomimic effort to make him understand this, I must have attracted the attention of this young fellow's wife or brother, for another squirrel came out of the same window of the same little house and joined us on the bench. I shrugged some more, and soon we were four, then five, then six, then seven—all from the same little house. It was quite like that hilarious clown act in the circus when twenty-seven odd clowns, midgets, and giants get out of an automobile one at a time. Two more came scurrying down. I thought that they must live in terribly close quarters in that boarding house. I wondered if they kept it clean. Perhaps they sleep out in the summer, I thought; and it must be quite cozy in winter, all lying down in a row with their own bushy tails spread over them like blankets. Boarding house, I thought. Why not a hotel? I wondered if anybody had ever thought of building a hotel for squirrels, a nice biggish sort of a Saratoga hotel with a comfortable porch all around it, big windows and doors, with large-size storage rooms for nuts upstairs. I suddenly had a delightful twinge in my old noggin. Why not *build one myself!* The idea excited me so much I could hardly wait to get started. I suppose another reason why I had never made models before was that it took time and I could find no real reason to do it. This, on the other hand, would occupy time, and I thought the purpose delightful. I apologized to the squirrels for my empty-handedness, promised to make it up to them, assured them that they would see more of me in the future, and practically ran all the way home."

"Where is Squirrel Hotel?" I asked.

"*Well hidden!*" he answered sharply.

I excused myself for the interruption, and the old man continued.

"I spent the entire night drawing up plans, slept all of the following morning, and bought the necessary materials for construction in the Land Room of my old store that afternoon. In four weeks of delightful labor, I built the hotel. I made it carefully in sections which fitted neatly and solidly together like a prefabricated house. I searched for days until I found a well-hidden spot, took the disassembled hotel to the spot in two trips, dug a nice flat foundation for it, lined it with stone and dug a trench around it for drainage. I assembled Squirrel Hotel.

"It looked perfectly charming in its natural setting. I baited it with nice fresh walnuts and hid behind a tree and waited. Squirrels soon came—first one at a time, then in packs. I watched them, delighted, as they walked into the entrance hall and up the stairs—that is, some of them used the main entrance, but most of them didn't seem to care whether they used doors or windows. I watched them come out on the upstairs porch and walk back inside. I saw them through the windows, eating nuts. Their curiosity was most diverting. I believe each squirrel made a complete tour of all of the rooms. They ran up and down the stairs, in and out of the windows and doors, around

28

and around the porches. *It works!* I thought. *It really works!*

"I waited around until nightfall to see how many were going to move in. Nightfall came, but, to my dismay, one by one the squirrels left the hotel and returned to their cramped little houses. This was awful! I wondered if their only interest in the place was in eating the nuts I had put there. I was feeling very sad. I went home and decided to come back the next day and see if they would go to Squirrel Hotel without a single nut in any of its rooms. I felt quite convinced they wouldn't.

"The next morning I was tickled to find that they had all returned and were playing in and out of it in hilarious fashion. I had to find out why they wouldn't stay there at night. What was it that made them prefer their old homes? I was determined to solve this problem."

"Did you?" I asked.

"Are you *really* interested?"

"Completely!" I said. "I'm absolutely fascinated."

"Then come back tomorrow, and I'll tell you more."

"You couldn't tell me more *now?*" I asked.

"Tomorrow," he said. He had risen from the bench and was shaking my hand. "Good-by," he said and walked off with his little stage under his arm. "By the way, tomorrow's concert is at nine o'clock."

"Morning or evening?"

"Evening," the old man said, "after dark."

29

THE THIRD DAY

The next evening I arrived at the park while there was still plenty of daylight. I was curious about this evening concert. I wondered how the old man was going to attract a crowd and how he would light up the little stage. I sat on the hillside overlooking the lake and awaited his arrival. He soon appeared and looked about him for what he thought would be a suitable spot for the concert. I thought of going down to help him set up the stage but then decided that he perhaps had a few surprises to spring this time, as he had the day before, and would be more annoyed than pleased by my presence.

Before his arrival I pictured him as picking a bench directly under a light, which to me seemed the ideal bright spot in which to attract a crowd and perform. I watched him as he stood near the lake, looking over the situation. Instead of picking my brightly lit bench, he chose one which was shaded by big trees and as dark as a coal bin.

The other two days I had arrived after the concert had started and had therefore not seen him come on the scene. This time I was able to clear up another question that had bothered me. I had been wondering how the bees lived in the stage when it was all folded up. The answer to this problem was ridiculously simple: he carried the stage under his arm, all opened out and ready for action. He only folded it up after the concert was finished and the bees had been dismissed.

He set the stage up on the shaded bench, and I was just barely able to see him lean over and peek under the tiny curtain to see if all was in order inside. As he did this, it seemed to me that a light from within lit up his face—not a steady light, but a firelight, as though he had looked into a red-hot stove. This was indeed puzzling!

He took his little easel out of his pocket and placed it on

31

one side of the stage. He had attached to it a little flashlight bulb with a small reflector. He tested the light. This bulb was lit by a battery which he carefully hid under the bench. He was now, I imagined, just about ready to perform; but how, I wondered, would he attract a crowd to the dismal spot he had chosen?

I saw him stick some sort of pegs in the ground in a circle all around the bench. He took out some matches and walked around lighting these objects. They were giant sparklers, and, before the last one had burned out, their charming dazzling and sizzling lights had attracted as big an audience as the old man could possibly handle. I quickly ran down the hill to assure myself of a good place near the curtain.

The old man waited until the crowd had quieted down and was giving him full attention. He then began his first Evening Concert. He dramatically opened up the rear curtain, the curtain behind the stage, from which point he directed the bee orchestra with rose and glove. He didn't open the front curtain at first. From inside the stage a brilliant flamelike light shone forth onto the old man's face, lighting it from underneath and casting deep shadows on his eyes. It was indeed as though his face were being lit by the roaring flames from a furnace fire. With this sinister light on his beaming face, he directed the bees in a few infernal selections from the opera *Faust*. The response to this overture was most gratifying.

It was a warm night, and this flamelike light gave forth an impression of almost unbearable heat. The old man next directed

"Glow, Little Glowworm," in the midst of which number he drew the front curtain, revealing the source of the flickering light. The sides and top of the stage were lined with hundreds of fireflies, separated from the bees by fine mosquito netting.

The concert was a great success, and after having released the fireflies, dismissed the bees, and folded the stage, the old man was most pleased to count up nineteen dollars and eighty-eight cents for still a new record.

We were alone on this darkest of benches, decidedly undisturbed, a perfect spot to get on with further details about Squirrel Hotel.

"Yesterday," I said, "you told me that the squirrels left Squirrel Hotel at night and that you were determined to find out why. How did you solve this problem and get the squirrels to live there night and day?"

"A woolly dog solved it for me," the old man said.

"A dog? How in the world did he do it?"

"Well, as I said yesterday, the squirrels seemed to love playing in the Hotel in the daytime—that is, all except one, who sat up in a tree, paying no attention to the Hotel but intently studying the surrounding landscape. I noticed this lone fellow after a while and wondered why he didn't join his friends in the fun. Suddenly, as I was watching him, he sent forth a rasping, piercing shriek, an angry sort of yelp followed by an even louder call. The Hotel was emptied at once; squirrels scrambled out of the doors and windows, tripped over each other in the panic,

33

leaped and bounded from the porches, and scurried full speed to the tops of the surrounding trees. Then there was complete silence. Just about half a minute later a shaggy dog made his appearance. Dogs are great enemies of squirrels. He looked at me in a bored sort of way, then sniffed the Hotel with considerable interest. His nose must have detected the recent presence of the squirrels. He looked into all the rooms, stuck his big nose in the entrance hall, sniffed loudly up the halls and stair wells, inspected the attic. Satisfied that the building was quite deserted, he cast his eyes on the surrounding treetops, then rather reluctantly left the scene. After another minute had gone by, the lookout squirrel—for that is exactly what the lone fellow was —gave an all-clear yelp, and the squirrels returned to their Hotel and continued playing. I at once realized why they didn't care to spend the night in Squirrel Hotel. How could they sleep peacefully on the ground at the mercy of any enemy animal who happened to wander by? The Hotel simply needed to be raised off the ground.

"It was too big to be put in a tall tree, and besides if I put it up in one it would be hard to keep it hidden. There are houses in some swampy areas in Africa which are built on stilts and thus raised above the soggy marshes. I got ahold of four stout posts, which I drove into the ground, and I moved Squirrel Hotel quite high up into the air. That night I was most pleased to discover as darkness came that no squirrel left Squirrel Hotel but, on the contrary, other squirrels climbed up the posts and entered it through the doors and windows. When I left, somewhere around midnight, the Hotel's accommodations were completely filled. The thing that touched me more than anything else that day was that, far from having liked Squirrel Hotel only for the nuts I had put into it, the squirrels dug up nuts from their own reserves, which they stored neatly in the attic. They seemed determined to stay a while."

"That's a very sweet story," I said. "I suppose there remains but one thing to tell me, and that's where I might find Squirrel Hotel. Where is it?"

"*Not so fast,* young man," he said. "Tell me, have you ever built models?"

"No, I can't say that I have."

"Exactly. If you had you would know full well that the excitement doesn't really begin until you start putting on the finishing touches. The big fun is at the end."

"What sort of finishing touches did you add?"

"Hotel finishing touches," he said. "Improvements. What is the first thing you see in big type when you read a hotel advertisement? 'ALL MODERN COMFORTS.' At first Squirrel Hotel was just a series of bare rooms and, as I soon found out, rather poorly planned."

"Did the squirrels dislike the floor plans?"

"They seemed to, and with apparent good reason. The air didn't circulate too well. They chewed new doors through several of the partitions and a couple of new windows through the

35

walls. My first job was to square off these holes and make them like the other windows and doors. The squirrels didn't seem to have much of an eye for décor."

"Did they mind your puttering around their building?"

"Not at all. They seemed to know I was their friend. I next got a few chairs to put in the rooms—tables too—and I put beds in the bedrooms. I knew they wouldn't use most of the furniture, but I thought it would improve the looks of the place. They slept in the beds. The furniture came from my old toy store. The Hotel looked like a summer hotel, so I put rocking chairs on the porches, country style."

"Did they use them?" I asked, imagining as I did a squirrel leaning back on his tail and furiously rocking back and forth.

"Never," he said. "I even had to nail them down to stop the squirrels from kicking them off the porch."

"Did they use the porches?"

"I'm glad you asked that," he said. "People on vacation in summer hotels sit on porches by the hour just to watch other people go by. I wondered what a squirrel would like to look at. There was not much of a view in my secret hiding spot. I suddenly remembered that animals like to look at themselves. I surrounded the Hotel with mirrors. They were fascinated by the sight of themselves running around the porches and in and out of the windows and doors. They watched themselves by the hour both from the porches and peering through the windows."

"Any other improvements?"

"Of course. I noticed that the squirrels had beaten a tiny path through the thick surrounding bushes. I squeezed my way through the path until I came to a small rushing stream of fresh water fed by a small spring. I piped some of this water through tiny pipes. I lined one of the rooms in the Hotel with zinc and made a small drain at the bottom of it, running through the floor. I fixed a continuous stream of water to run through that room; it was always about an inch and a half deep. They now had a continuous supply of fresh water to drink and a place big enough to bathe in if they cared to, though I never saw any of them try it.

"Then too, discovering that spring opened up a whole new set of possibilities. I made a small dam in it and sent the stream splashing over a water wheel. I attached the water wheel to an electric generator, and I now had enough power to operate a little electric motor. I spent so much time at my old toy store that I'm certain my former salesmen thought I had gone completely crazy. I could have wired the Hotel and put flashlight bulbs in every room for light, and a little electric sign outside, but at the time I didn't think the squirrels could be taught how to turn the lights on and off. I had to think of a silent undisturbing use for this electric power that could run day and night without being turned off or bothering the squirrels. After thinking of every possibility, I happened on the idea of an escalator— a rather silly idea, but one which I found amusing. With considerable difficulty, and after several false starts, I made one.

I placed it between the top floor and the attic. I thought that if by some chance they liked this first one I would install them on the two other floors. Well, they never used it in the ordinary way, but they did seem to enjoy it. Two of the squirrels invented a game which was played by the hour. One of them would go up to the attic and send a nut bouncing down the escalator. The other would stand at the bottom, run and pick up the nut, put it on the escalator, and watch it go back up to the attic, where the other would bounce it down again. I thought that was as good a use as any, but decided that one escalator was enough for Squirrel Hotel."

I laughed at this new use for escalators, then told the old man that it was too bad about the electric lights. I imagined that Squirrel Hotel would have looked lovely all lit up at night.

"I thought so too," said the old man, "and managed also to solve this situation. I noticed in pet shops that squirrels seemed to enjoy running around in squirrel cages. I added a big one to Squirrel Hotel, with an entrance to it from the downstairs porch. They used it a great deal for exercise. To this wheel I attached another small electric generator, the power from which was used to light up the rooms. Since they didn't use the wheel after bedtime, the lights went out at that time, and not one of them was kept awake by them.

"That's about all there is to it," said the old man. "It does have a lightning rod. Then too, as the very last finishing touch I added a spiral-shaped slide leading down to the ground. I

SQUIRREL HOTEL

William Pène du Bois

noticed on my circus tour that bears like to slide down slides very much. I thought squirrels might like them too. I also thought this slide might make a good fire escape in case the Hotel should catch on fire due to some small short circuit. I made it and attached it. A few of the squirrels use it every day."

"Now one more thing," I asked. "You said yesterday that when you ran out of money and had no place to sleep the squirrels helped you keep alive. How did they do that?"

"Well, it wasn't a very elegant sort of life, but the Hotel is in a well-hidden sheltered spot. I slept under the Hotel, between the four posts, and I kept alive by eating nuts, which by then were fairly bursting out of the attic. At no time, I am pleased to say, did they mind my presence or did they resent feeding me.

"I wonder," the old man said, "if now that you know all about it you are still *really* interested in seeing it, managing it, keeping it in good running order?"

"*More so than ever!*" I shouted.

"Excellent," he said, "very good. Young man, come and see me again tomorrow. I shall take you to Squirrel Hotel and turn the place over to you."

We shook hands and said good night. On my way home I suddenly remembered that I had forgotten to ask him whether the next day's concert would be in the afternoon or evening. I decided to return to the park in the afternoon. I would wait for him if he had planned another night concert.

THE FOURTH DAY

Upon reaching the top of the hill overlooking the lake in the park the following afternoon, I was most pleased to see a little group of people surrounding someone on a bench. I hurried down to the spot and gently made my way through the crowd, thinking as I did this that the old man would never beat the attendance record with this little group.

I was terribly disappointed to find that instead of its being my friend with the Bee's Orchestra they were watching, it was one of those strange old mechanics with a remarkable home-made steamboat. I quickly looked at the other benches around the lake and just as quickly found them all to be quite empty.

It was the usual time for his afternoon concert to be in full swing, so I decided that he must again be planning on an evening program. Having decided before to wait for him in the park, I spent a good deal of the rest of the afternoon examining the model boat. It was an old sidewheeler with SHOWBOAT written in brilliant letters on its sides. I was so full of thoughts of Squirrel Hotel that I could look upon this fine model only as an ideal boat for Sunday outings for the furry animals. This was a foolish notion, for I am certain that squirrels couldn't stand being that near the water.

I waited patiently as the Sterno fire built up steam in the boilers. I watched the old mechanic test the amount of steam by tooting the whistles and checking the tiny pressure gauges. Finally the sidewheels started to turn, first with noisy gasps of hesitation, then full speed, shaking the whole boat. The crowd eagerly followed the old mechanic to the edge of the lake. He carefully placed SHOWBOAT in the water. The boat chugged ahead a foot or two and then stopped. This usually happens with model steamboats; the coolness of the water lowers the steam pressure. The old man hauled it back to shore with a long broomstick which had a hook on one end and a rubber tip

on the other. He took it back to his bench and waited for more pressure to build up.

When the boilers seemed ready to explode, he returned to the lake for a new launching. The SHOWBOAT bravely headed out full steam for the open seas. It seemed to pick up speed as it pushed forward.

Way out in the middle of the lake it met another far less imposing but equally brave little homemade ship. This one was a mere pointed piece of board with a pencil stuck in a knothole amidships. The pencil was woven through a sheet of ruled yellow paper.

The two boats sideswiped each other, and somehow one of the sidewheels of the steamship managed to roll right up on the deck of the sailboat. There it hit the mast and came to a stop. The steam pressure was thus all concentrated on the other sidewheel, which started to whirl away full blast. The two boats went into a fast spin way out in the middle of the lake. This nautical waltz got them nowhere. The old mechanic started pulling his hair.

The two boats went round and round for twenty full minutes, until finally the SHOWBOAT ran out of steam. Only then, maddeningly, did it slip off the sailboat's deck. The sailboat, with the help of a light breeze, quickly gained shore, where it found no one interested enough in it to greet its arrival. The SHOWBOAT waited fifteen full minutes while the old mechanic threw a lead sinker which was attached to a fish line across its bow and towed it shamefully back to shore. I watched the old mechanic as he took it all apart and dried it all, bit by bit, ever so carefully. As he left for home, the sun was setting, and I knew it wouldn't be long before a new Bee Orchestra would be making its one and only appearance.

As I sat waiting, I thought to myself that the old man would of course perform at night the day he was to take me to Squirrel Hotel. He was so determined to keep its hiding place secret, he wouldn't think of taking me there in full daylight. I was sorry I'd been so stupid as not to have thought of this earlier.

It was soon quite dark, and I kept my eyes fixed on the well-shaded bench. The old man didn't show up.

He's late, I thought. He's had trouble with the bees.

I waited another full hour. I kept walking to the top of the hill and scanning the park all around me for any signs of twinkling sparklers. There was nothing but the usual darkness. At ten o'clock the park was much too deserted for the old man to gather the smallest of crowds. I decided to go home. I returned to the park every day and night for two full weeks. I thought that maybe he was testing my interest in Squirrel Hotel to some fantastic extreme.

I never saw the old man again.

Three weeks after the last time I'd seen him I decided to do some detective work. I was sincerely worried about the old fellow, but also had a terrible notion that maybe he'd made up the whole idea of Squirrel Hotel. I imagined that he didn't tell me all about it the first day because he hadn't figured out the whole extraordinary place in his mind. Here was a tale which was such an enormous fib that it took him three full days to make it up. I decided to pay a visit to Land, Sea & Air, Inc.

I approached the store with mixed feelings. I hoped that they would give me information which would help prove the existence of Squirrel Hotel, but then I also rather hoped that they wouldn't. If I found out that the Hotel existed, this would surely mean that something was wrong with the old man, for what possible reason could he have for not showing up and taking me to it after promising me that he would? I hated to think that something might have happened to him.

He certainly hadn't lied when he told me about the store. It was exactly as he had described it, and most handsome. I walked into the Land Room, where I found a rather elderly gentleman, perhaps the new owner. I asked him if he knew the former owner of the store. I realized suddenly that I had never thought to ask the old man his name.

"Mr. Leonard Schurman," he said, smiling. "Yes, certainly."

"Have you seen him lately?"

"No. That is not *too* recently. It seems to me he was here about six weeks or so ago."

45

"What did he want?"

"Why do you ask?" he said. "Is there something wrong with him?"

"I don't know," I said. "That's more or less what I'm trying to find out."

"I see. Well, he came to see us then about an antique marionette stage he'd bought in Paris a couple of years before. He had hoped we'd be able to sell it for him, but we hadn't. He came to pick it up and take it home."

"For the Bee's Orchestra!" I said.

"What's that?"

"Oh, nothing. Had you seen him before—that is, since he sold the store?"

"Not recently. There was a time we all well remember, a little over two years ago, I believe, when we had a spell of seeing him just about every day for two months. He bought nearly enough stuff to start a new little store. We frankly thought he was a little out of his mind—second childhood or something."

"Could you possibly show me a list of the things he bought?"

"We have a record of it, of course, but it seems a rather strange request. What do you want to know all this for?"

"I can assure you, sir," I said, "that I have nothing more than the old man's welfare in mind. He seems to have disappeared. This might possibly help me find him."

"I'm sorry," he said. "We shall of course do all we can to

help. It will take a little while to dig up the old sales slips. Would you please come back tomorrow morning?"

I assured him that I would.

The sales slips proved to make an extraordinary list. Here are a few of the items mentioned, all of which the salesman described as being, of course, in miniature:

48 four-poster canopied beds

48 tables, small

8 tables, dining-room

150 chairs, straight, American Colonial

24 rocking chairs, ladderback

32 pairs of curtains

1 gross flashlight bulbs

2 electric motors, Meccano

3 generators, Meccano

32 venetian blinds

100 assorted paintings

48 awnings, striped

6 American flags

Those were but a few of the things listed. From the Sea Room there was mention of a purchase of forty-eight hammocks. I pictured these as being strung up in the trees surrounding Squirrel Hotel for summer napping.

I have looked carefully through the park for Squirrel Hotel, but I very much regret to say that I haven't found it yet. I have thought of many things which might possibly make it hard to find, one of which is that the mirrors which surround the Hotel might have been double-faced. If this were true, I might have looked directly at the site of the Hotel and seen nothing but the reflection of the surrounding trees, bushes, and leaves. I wouldn't put this trick past the old man's imagination.

I haven't seen or heard of the old man or of the Bee's Orchestra.

This to me is indeed sad.

Just one more thing:

If someone had told me of the Bee's Orchestra and of Squirrel Hotel I feel certain that I would have found it far easier to believe in the existence of Squirrel Hotel.

But *I have seen* the Bee's Orchestra!

Please help me find Squirrel Hotel, or if you have seen it, please tell me where it is. It most probably needs a good deal of attention and care, and I *am* supposed to be the person left in charge.

ANN A. Flowers, Patricia Lord, and Betsy Groban edited the introductory material in this book, which was phototypeset on a Mergenthaler 606-CRT typesetter in Primer and Primer Italic typefaces by Trade Composition of Springfield, MA. This book was printed and bound by Braun-Brumfield, Inc. of Ann Arbor, Michigan.

Gregg Press
Children's Literature Series
Ann A. Flowers and
Patricia Lord, *Editors*

When Jays Fly to Bárbmo by Margaret
Balderson. New Introduction by Anne Izard.

Cautionary Tales by Hilaire Belloc. New
Introduction by Sally Holmes Holtze.

The Hurdy-Gurdy Man by Margery Williams
Bianco. New Introduction by
Mary M. Burns.

Nurse Matilda by Christianna Brand. New
Introduction by Sally Holmes Holtze.

Azor and the Blue-Eyed Cow by Maude
Crowley. New Introduction by
Eunice Blake Bohanon.

The Village That Slept by Monique Peyrouton
de Ladebat. New Introduction by
Charlotte A. Gallant.

Squirrel Hotel by William Pène du Bois. New
Introduction by Paul Heins.

The Boy Jones by Patricia Gordon. New
Introduction by Lois Winkel.

The Little White Horse by Elizabeth Goudge.
New Introduction by Kate M. Flanagan.

The Minnow Leads to Treasure by A. Philippa Pearce. New Introduction by Ethel Heins.

The Maplin Bird by K. M. Peyton. New Introduction by Karen M. Klockner.

Ounce, Dice, Trice by Alastair Reid. New Introduction by Elizabeth Johnson.

The Sea of Gold and Other Tales from Japan by Yoshiko Uchida. New Introduction by Marcia Brown.

Dear Enemy by Jean Webster. New Introduction by Ann A. Flowers.

Mistress Masham's Repose by T. H. White. New Introduction by Ann A. Flowers.